# Chick and Brain
# Egg or Eyeball?

### Cece Bell

CANDLEWICK PRESS

# CONTENTS

# Chapter 1
# Egg or Eyeball?

4

8

10

14

# Chapter 2
# Spot

19

22

23

24

# Chapter 3
# Puff

37

39

46

47

# Chapter 4
# Something Else

57

Oh, Kelli Huffman!
Oh, Frank Huffman!
Oh, oh, oh!
This book is for you.

First edition 2020

Library of Congress Catalog Card Number pending
ISBN 978-1-5362-0439-1

19 20 21 22 23 24 LEO 10 9 8 7 6 5 4 3 2 1

Printed in Heshan, Guangdong, China

This book was typeset in JHA My Happy 70s.
The illustrations were created in watercolor and ink.

Candlewick Press
99 Dover Street
Somerville, Massachusetts 02144

visit us at www.candlewick.com